KICK, PASS, AND RUN

story and pictures by

Leonard Kessler

HarperTrophy
A Division of HarperCollins*Publishers*

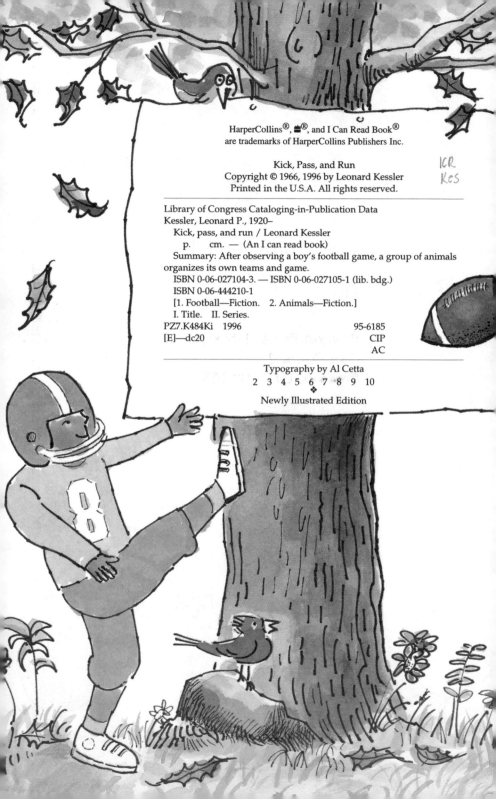

Kick, Pass, and Run
Copyright © 1966, 1996 by Leonard Kessler
Printed in the U.S.A. All rights reserved.

Library of Congress Cataloging-in-Publication Data
Kessler, Leonard P., 1920–
  Kick, pass, and run / Leonard Kessler
    p.   cm. — (An I can read book)
  Summary: After observing a boy's football game, a group of animals
organizes its own teams and game.
  ISBN 0-06-027104-3. — ISBN 0-06-027105-1 (lib. bdg.)
  ISBN 0-06-444210-1
  [1. Football—Fiction.   2. Animals—Fiction.]
  I. Title.   II. Series.
PZ7.K484Ki   1996   95-6185
[E]—dc20   CIP
                                                          AC

Typography by Al Cetta
2   3   4   5   6   7   8   9   10
❖
Newly Illustrated Edition

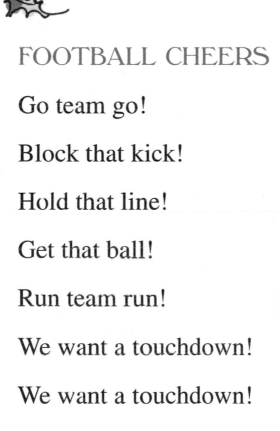

FOOTBALL CHEERS

Go team go!

Block that kick!

Hold that line!

Get that ball!

Run team run!

We want a touchdown!

We want a touchdown!

FOOTBALL WORDS

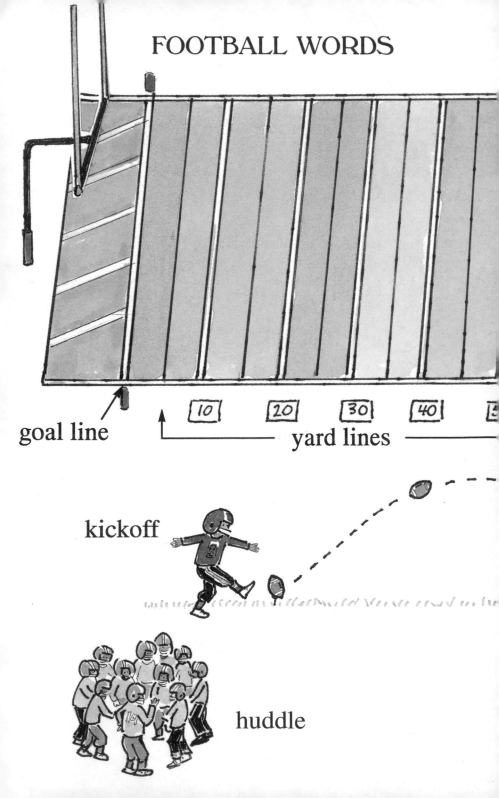

goal line

10 20 30 40 5

yard lines

kickoff

huddle

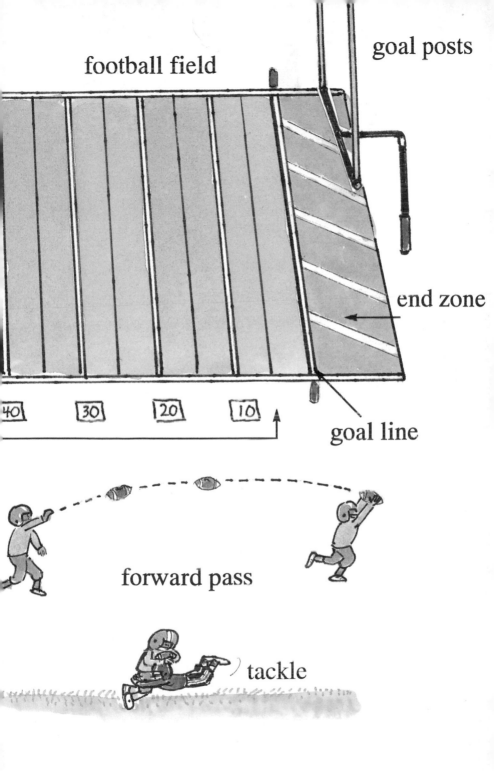

football field

goal posts

end zone

40 30 20 10

goal line

forward pass

tackle

Rabbit was

the first one

to *hear* it.

Duck was

the first one

to *see* it.

Cat was

the first one

to *feel* it.

"What is it?"

asked Dog.

Owl said,

"It's an egg!"

"An egg?" asked Frog.

"Yes, an egg," said Owl.

"It's an elephant's egg!"

"No," said Turtle.

"An elephant's egg

is not brown."

Owl said, "It is

a brown bear's egg."

"Bears do not lay eggs,"

said Duck.

She laughed.

"I can tell an egg

when I see one.

And that is *not* an egg!"

14

"Shhh," said Cat.

"Someone is coming!"

They all hid.

"Here it is,"

said a boy.

"Here is our

FOOTBALL!"

16

"It's a football,"

said Owl.

"What is a football?"

asked Frog.

17

"A football

is a football,"

said Owl.

"Let's follow that boy,"

said Dog.

18

They went up the hill.

"Shhh. Be quiet,"

said Owl.

"Let's see how they play

with the football."

19

They saw two teams

on the football field.

One team was the Jets.

One team was the Giants.

"I am for the Jets,"

said Duck.

"I am for the Giants,"

said Rabbit.

"I am for *quiet*!"

said Owl.

21

"Ready for the kickoff,"

yelled the Giants' kicker.

He kicked the football.

Up it went in the air.

22

A Jets' player

caught the football.

He ran up the field.

"Stop him! Tackle him!"

yelled the Giants.

"Wow," said Duck,

"that looks like fun."

She tackled Rabbit.

"Stop that," said Cat.

24

The Jets went into a huddle.

"The fullback

will carry the ball

around left end,"

said the quarterback.

Out of the huddle came the Jets.

"First down and ten yards to go,"

said the Jets' quarterback.

"Ready . . . Set . . . Down . . .

Hup 1 . . . Hup 2 . . . Hup 3."

The center gave him the ball.

"Hup 1 . . . Hup 2 . . . Hup 3.

Hup 1 . . . Hup 2 . . . Hup 3,"

quacked Duck.

"Oh, stop that,"

said Owl.

The quarterback

flipped the football

to the fullback.

The fullback ran five yards

before the Giants tackled him.

"Go, team, go!" quacked Duck.

Out of the huddle

came the Jets again.

"Second down

and five yards to go,"

said the quarterback.

"Ready . . . Set . . . Down . . .

Hup 1 . . . Hup 2 . . . Hup 3."

He took the ball.

Back he went.

Back. Back.

"Look out for a forward pass,"

yelled the Giants.

"Look out for a forward pass!"

yelled Frog.

Up in the air

went the football.

Down it came

to the Jets' receiver.

He caught the ball

and ran

and ran

and ran

all the way

into the end zone.

"It's a TOUCHDOWN!

A TOUCHDOWN!

Six points for our team,"

yelled the Jets.

"It's a touchdown,"

yelled Turtle.

"Wow," said Duck.

"He made a touchdown."

"What's a touchdown?"
asked Frog.

"A touchdown is six points,"
said Owl.

"Let's play football,"
said Cat.

"Yes," said Duck.

"I want to make
a touchdown."

Away they ran—

back into the woods.

"Here is a good spot

to play," said Turtle.

"Let's choose teams,"

said Owl.

"Dog, Cat, Rabbit,

Turtle, and Frog

will be the Giants.

And *my* team

will be the Jets—

Duck, the three

little birds, and me!"

37

"That Owl," said Turtle,

"is such a big boss."

"Oh, forget it," said Dog.

"Let's play football."

"But we need a football,"

said Frog.

"How about an apple?"

said Owl.

"No, thanks," said Frog.

"I'm not hungry."

"How about an apple

for a football?" said Owl.

"An apple will be fine,"

said Duck.

"Let's play football!"

"Kickoff," said Owl.

Up went the apple.

Rabbit caught it and ran.

He ran fast.

Duck tackled him.

The Giants went

into a huddle.

"Frog will carry the ball

around left end,"

Dog said softly.

42

Out of the huddle

came the Giants.

"First down

and ten yards to go,"

said Dog.

"Ready . . . Set . . . Down . . .

Hup 1 . . . Hup 2 . . . Hup 3."

He got the apple.

He gave it to Cat,

who gave it to Rabbit,

who gave it to Frog.

All the Jets

jumped on Frog.

44

"Who has the apple?"

asked Owl.

"Not me," said Rabbit.

"Not me," said Cat.

"Not me," said Dog.

"No. Not me," said Turtle.

They all looked at Frog.

"I guess I *was* hungry,"

said Frog.

"You ATE THE FOOTBALL?"

said Duck.

"Now we need

a new football."

46

"How about

this paper bag?"

asked Owl.

"We can blow it up.

That will make

a good football."

Puff. Puff. Puff.

He blew up the bag.

"Tie it with this string,"

said Rabbit.

"Some football,"

said Duck.

"It's our turn

to get the ball,"

said Owl.

"Ready . . . Set . . . Down . . ."

"Hop 1 . . . Hop 2," quacked Duck.

"Not Hop," said Owl. "It's Hup."

"Up?" said Duck.

She took the ball

and up in the air she flew.

"No fair! No fair!"

yelled Rabbit.

"You can't fly!

Only the ball

can go in the air."

50

"Yes, I can," said Duck.

"No, you can't."

"Yes, I can,

you stupid Rabbit."

"No, you can't,

you silly Duck."

"Oh, oh. Another fight,"

said Frog.

"Stop it! Stop it!" said Owl.

"That's not the way

to play football."

"Then I won't play,"

said Duck.

"Oh, let her go,"

said Turtle.

"But we *need* her,"

said Dog.

"The teams won't be even."

"Come back and play.

We need you," said Owl.

"Okay," said Duck.

She picked up

the paper-bag football.

"Let's see how far I can

kick it," said Duck.

"DON'T KICK

THE PAPER BAG!"

shouted Owl.

But it was too late.

Up went the bag.

"No more football," said Dog.

"That's the end of the game,"

said Turtle.

Whissh!

Rabbit was the first one

to *hear* it.

Duck was the first one

to *see* it.

And Cat was the first one

to *catch* it!

"It's a REAL FOOTBALL!"

he shouted.

And away he went.

"Tackle him!"

yelled Owl.

"Stop him! Stop him!"

quacked Duck.

But they did not

catch him.

He ran

and ran

and ran.

61

"Touchdown!"

"Six points

for the Giants!"

Rabbit hopped

up and down.

"Look out!

Someone is coming,"

shouted Frog.

Cat dropped the football.

They all hid.

"Here it is,"

said the boy.

"Here is our football.

how it got

here?"